This book belongs to...

Jasper's Beanstalk

Nick Butterworth and Mick Inkpen

Hodder
Children's
Books

A division of Hachette Children's Books

On Monday
Jasper found
a bean.

On Tuesday
he planted it.

On Wednesday he watered it.

On Thursday
he dug and raked
and sprayed and
hoed it.

On Friday night he picked

up all the slugs and snails.

On Saturday he even mowed it!

On Sunday
Jasper waited
and waited
and waited...

When Monday
came around again
he dug it up.

'That bean
will never make
a beanstalk,'
said Jasper.

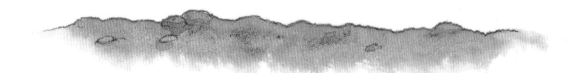

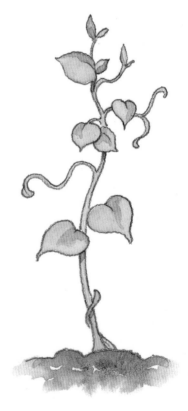

But a long, long,

long   time   later...

It did!

(It was on a Thursday, I think.)

Now Jasper is looking for giants!

First published in 1992 by Hodder Children's Books

This edition published in 2008

Copyright © Nick Butterworth and Mick Inkpen 1992

Hodder Children's Books
338 Euston Road, London NW1 3BH

Hodder Children's Books Australia
Level 17/207 Kent Street, Sydney, NSW 2000

The right of Nick Butterworth and Mick Inkpen to be identified
as the author and illustrator of this Work has been asserted by them
in accordance with the Copyright, Designs and Patents Act 1988.

A catalogue record of this book is available
from the British Library.

ISBN: 978 0 340 94511 7

Printed in China
Hodder Children's Books is a division of Hachette Children's Books,
an Hachette Livre UK Company